An ARTHUR

ARTHUR
AND THE
CRUNCH CEREAL CONTEST

Other ARTHUR Readers
by Marc Brown

Arthur's Mystery Envelope

Arthur and the
Scare-Your-Pants-Off Club

Arthur Accused!

Arthur Locked in the Library!

Arthur's Dino Dilemma

MARC BROWN

ARTHUR
AND THE
CRUNCH CEREAL CONTEST

RED FOX

For Eliza

A Red Fox Book

Published by Random House Children's Books
20 Vauxhall Bridge Road, London SW1V 2SA

A division of The Random House Group Ltd
London Melbourne Sydney Auckland
Johannesburg and agencies throughout the world

Text by Stephen Kerensky, based on the teleplay by Tom Hirsch

First published in the United States of America by Little, Brown & Company, and
simultaneously in Canada by Little, Brown & Company (Canada) Limited 1998

Red Fox edition 1999

3 5 7 9 10 8 6 4

Printed and bound in Great Britain by Bookmarque Ltd, Croydon, Surrey

Papers used by The Random House Group Limited are natural, recyclable products made
from wood grown in sustainable forest. The manufacturing processes conform to the
environmental regulations of the country of origin.

THE RANDOM HOUSE GROUP Limited Reg. No. 954009

ISBN 0 09 940323 4

Chapter 1

• • • • • • • • • •

'A touch of cinnamon . . . a hint of brown sugar . . . just a suspicion of cloves.'

Mr Read stood in front of the cooker, bringing his latest creation to life. The steam from the pot swirled up towards the frosted window.

'Yes, siree, on a chilly morning like this, everyone needs some porridge that will really stick to your ribs.'

He swivelled around quickly, presenting a steaming pot.

The rest of the family were sitting at the table.

'I'm not very hungry this morning,'

said Arthur.

'Me, neither,' said D.W.

Only baby Kate looked pleased. She liked playing with porridge. It always ended up in the most interesting places.

'Now, now,' said their mother. 'Your father's been working hard on this. Let's give it a chance.'

'Thank you, dear,' said Mr Read. 'And in recognition of your support, we'll start with a nice healthy portion for you.'

He tilted the pot and tried to spoon some into her bowl. But nothing came out. The porridge had hardened like cement.

'Hmmm...' Mr Read looked puzzled. 'The baking powder must have reacted with the molasses...'

'Oh, that's terrible!' said Mrs Read. From the look on her face, though, it didn't appear as if she minded at all.

'That was *close*', whispered D.W.

Arthur nodded.

'Looks like we'll have to make do with normal cereal,' said Mrs Read. 'Arthur, would you —'

'Sure, Mom!' Arthur got up to get the cereal from the cabinet.

Mr Read put the pot in the sink. 'We'll have to bury this later – with full military honours, of course.'

Arthur opened the box of Crunch cereal. It was his favourite.

His father shook his head. 'I don't understand the appeal of that sugar-coated cardboard. Believe me, all you'll get from that stuff is a mouthful of fillings.'

'We're willing to take that risk,' said D.W.

As Arthur shook out a serving, an envelope fell out of the box into his bowl.

'Wow!' said D.W. 'And I thought letters only came in alphabet soup.'

Arthur opened the envelope and read the note inside aloud.

'Welcome to the Crunch Cereal Jingle Contest. Send us your song – and you could win a year's supply of Crunch cereal.'

Mr Read shook his head. 'I'll bet second place is a two-year supply.'

Arthur kept reading.

'The winning jingle will also be aired on TV in the new Crunch cereal advert. So don't just stand there, start crunching.'

'If we won that contest,' said D.W., 'we'd be famous.'

'There's something here in the small print,' said Arthur. 'Include twenty box-tops with each entry.' He sighed. 'That's a lot of crunching.'

'Isn't there something about "Void where prohibited by law"?' asked Mr Read.

Arthur looked. 'I don't think so,' he said.

'Good,' said D.W.

Arthur dumped some cereal in her bowl. 'I'm glad you feel that way. If you want to be famous start eating.'

Chapter 2

• • • • • • • • • • • •

Over the next few days, Arthur thought about jingles while brushing his teeth.

Crunch, crunch.

He thought about them while having a bath.

Crunch, crunch, crunch.

He even thought about them while doing his homework.

Crunch, crunch, crunch, crunch.

But none of this thinking got him very far. Wanting to write a jingle was a lot easier than actually making one up.

'Arthur, you need to get some fresh air,'

said his mother. 'Go outside and play.'

'I can't, Mom. The deadline is getting closer.'

'Sometimes, it's good to take a break,' said Mrs Read. 'Recharge your creative batteries. Clear your head. Why don't you go and make a snowman?'

'I don't think —'

'Move it,' said his mother. 'That's an order.'

Arthur went outside, but he wasn't happy about it. He started rolling a giant snowball. Then he started chipping pieces out of it.

The snowball was beginning to look like a giant piece of Crunch cereal.

'Is that what I think it is?'

D.W. had come outside, too. She shook her head at Arthur's snow sculpture.

'Mom wants me to clear my head,' he explained. 'I was hoping this would help.'

'You're in a rut, Arthur,' said D.W. 'You need to think harder.'

'I'm trying,' Arthur insisted. 'I've never thought so hard in my life.'

'Well, it doesn't show much. Maybe I could help.'

'We've been over this, D.W. You have your job.'

'I know, I know. I'm supposed to eat the cereal.'

Arthur nodded. 'Don't forget that.'

'Forget it?' said D.W. 'How could I? You put boxes in my bed, my toy chest, and my wardrobe. Everywhere I go, Crunch cereal is waiting for me.'

'Don't complain,' said Arthur. 'I'm eating it, too. And I've still got the hard part to deal with.'

D.W. was not impressed. 'You don't seem to be doing very well. Have you tried *dunce*? That sort of rhymes with *crunch*.'

'Sort of? I don't think the Crunch cereal people are looking for *sort of*. They're looking for rhythm. They're looking for poetry —'

'They're looking for a way to sell more cereal,' said D.W.

Arthur shook his head. 'You just don't have the right attitude. It's not surprising. You're too young to understand great art.'

D.W. laughed. 'I may not know great art, but I know what I like.'

'We're not talking about ice cream flavours here, D.W. A jingle has to be the perfect combination of words with the perfect melody.'

'Well, what about *lunch*?' said D.W. 'That rhymes with *crunch*.'

Arthur looked at the sky and sighed. Why couldn't inspiration hit him like a flash of lightning? He was ready. He was waiting.

A snowball hit him in the chest.

'Bull's-eye!' cried D.W.

'I'll bull's-eye you right back,' said Arthur.

He scooped up some snow and threw it back.

For that moment, at least, his head was clear.

Chapter 3

• • • • • • • • • • •

The school music room was empty except for Arthur. All the other kids were outside at break, running around and playing in the snow.

Arthur was trying out notes at the piano.

Dooonnng!

'Too low,' thought Arthur. 'Too sad.'

He tried a high note.

Diiiiink.

'Too silly,' thought Arthur.

He played a note in between.

Diiinnnng.

Arthur nodded. It was a start.

The door to the music room banged open.

'How's your jingle coming along, Arthur?' asked Buster. His face was red. Melting snow was dripping off his coat.

'I've pretty much finished the words.'

'Let's hear them,' said Buster.

Arthur cleared his throat.

'Eat Crunch,' he said.

Buster waited. But Arthur seemed to be done.

'Is there more?' he asked.

'No, that's it,' said Arthur. 'What do you think?'

Buster thought it over. 'It's short,' he decided.

'Short and sweet,' said Arthur. 'Just like the cereal.'

'Makes sense to me,' said Buster. 'I like it. So can you come out and play now?'

'I need more than words,' said Arthur.

'I need a tune to go with it. But I haven't had much luck . . .'

'Hmmmm,' said Buster. He looked at Arthur sitting alone at the piano. 'Maybe you should think bigger.'

'What would be bigger?'

'You know, more people, more instruments.'

Arthur liked the idea.

'If you had more musicians,' Buster went on, 'it would be easy to come up with a tune.'

'More musicians?' said Arthur. 'You mean, like a band?'

'You can have auditions and everything,' said Buster. 'We could check in the playground. I'll bet lots of kids would be interested.'

Arthur grabbed his coat. 'OK,' he said. 'Let's find out.'

The school playground was filled with bundled-up kids running around and making a lot of noise.

'Hi, Francine!' said Buster.

She was standing over a fallen pile of snow.

'It would have been beautiful,' she sighed.

'Arthur has a question for you,' said Buster.

'The snow sculpture to end all snow sculptures. It was bold. It was daring.'

'I was wondering, Francine . . .' Arthur began.

'But I couldn't do it by myself. I needed the help of my friends. And were they here for me?' She looked up at Arthur and Buster. 'No, they were inside doing some stupid thing instead.' She folded her arms. 'I don't think I'll ever be able to forgive them.'

19

'That's too bad,' said Arthur. 'Come on, Buster, we don't want to ask her at a time like this. She's in too much pain.'

'Ask me? Ask me what?'

'Arthur wants you to be in his band,' said Buster.

Francine's eyes widened. 'A band? I get to play my drums?'

'You would,' said Arthur. 'But since you're feeling so bad . . .'

Francine looked back at the fallen pile of snow. She gave it a kick. 'Oh, well,' she said. 'Easy come, easy go.' She turned back to Arthur.

'So, when do we start?'

Chapter 4

• • • • • • • • • • •

Arthur walked to the middle of the huge concert hall and stared out at the lights. He knew the audience was there, even if he couldn't see them. These were the country's greatest music critics. They had all come to hear his band play the Crunch cereal jingle.

Arthur spoke into the microphone. 'Ladies and gentlemen, there's been a change in the programme,' he announced. 'As you can see, I don't have a complete band yet. But Buster, Francine, and I will gladly —'

The audience started to boo. They had flown in from all over the country to hear the full band, not a few instruments patched together.

'Don't waste our time!'

'Get off the stage!'

'Come back when you're really ready!'

Arthur held up his hands. 'If I could just explain —' he began.

'Hey, Arthur!' said Buster. 'Snap out of it!'

Arthur blinked. He looked around his living room. 'I'm snapping,' I'm snapping,' he said.

'What's the matter?' Buster asked. 'You look worried.'

'Well, I am, a little. What if nobody comes today? What if they just ignored my signs about auditioning?'

'Um, Arthur, I don't think that will be a problem. Look!'

Outside the Read garage, a long line of kids had formed. Each of them was holding an instrument.

'Great!' said Arthur. 'Let's get started.'

As Buster took charge of the line,

Mr Read came out to see what was going on.

Buster explained why all the kids were there.

Mr Read looked relieved. 'Oh, it's that cereal business. Well, this is certainly ambitious.' He paused. 'Are we expected to feed everyone?'

'Oh, no,' said Buster. Arthur has that all taken care of.

Inside the garage, Arthur had put out bowls of Crunch cereal.

'Eat up, eat up!' he said. 'There's plenty for everyone.'

After a few minutes of crunching, the auditions began.

Sue Ellen was first. She played a riff of notes on her saxophone.

'Good,' said Arthur. 'But did I hear something rattling?'

'I think some of the Crunch cereal fell into my horn.'

'Well, try and blow it out. Next!'

Arthur listened to kids with banjos and piccolos, oboes and kazoos. One kid blew such a long note on his trumpet that he almost fainted.

The best part was when Grandma Thora arrived.

'Heard about the auditions,' she said. 'No special treatment for me. Don't even think about all the cakes I've baked over the years. And never mind about the chicken soup, either. Just listen.'

And with that, she pulled out a harmonica and began to play.

The jazzy notes drew everyone's attention. And then she sang: 'Grandma's got a brand-new bag! Gonna groove it all night long . . .'

Arthur was impressed. 'You're hired!' he said.

The last person in the line was Binky Barnes.

'You ready?' he asked.

Arthur nodded.

'Solo for clarinet by some old dead guy.'

Binky played a complicated series of notes.

Arthur's mouth dropped open.

'Wow!' said Buster. 'That was beautiful!'

Binky stalked up to him. 'Yeah, yeah, yeah . . . So am I in or not?'

'Absolutely!' said Arthur. 'Well, on one condition . . .'

'Which is?'

'That you help me finish the last box of Crunch.,'

Binky smiled. 'It's a deal,' he said.

Chapter 5

• • • • • • • • • • • •

Arthur stood in front of the newly formed Crunch Bunch band. Besides Buster and Francine, it included Binky, Muffy, the Brain, Sue Ellen, Prunella, and Grandma Thora.

'Where should *I* go?' D.W. asked.

She was standing by the door.

Arthur walked over to her. 'Auditions are over, D.W. Besides, you don't even play an instrument.'

'Don't worry. I don't want to play. I just want to be in charge.'

'That position is filled,' Arthur said firmly. He opened the door. 'I think I hear

Nadine calling you.' Nadine was D.W.'s invisible friend. 'She sounds like she's stuck in a snowdrift. You'd better check.'

'Hmmph!' muttered D.W. 'Big brothers can be so bossy.'

Arthur closed the door behind her and walked back to the others.

'Now, where were we? Oh, yes... I want to start with a bang. So everyone should play a real loud note. Then I'll —'

'Could we —' Francine began.

Arthur stared at her. 'Excuse me. Does someone have a question? I don't see anyone raising a hand.'

Francine rolled her eyes and raised her hand.

'Yes, Francine?'

'I just thought it might be nice to start off with a drum roll. For dramatic impact.'

'Yeah,' said Muffy, putting her violin under her chin. 'Followed by some strings.'

She started playing, and the Brain started plucking his cello.

'Then we'll add the horns,' said Sue Ellen. She blew into her saxophone while Prunella raised her trumpet.

'No,' said Arthur.

Everyone kept playing.

Arthur waved his arms. 'No! NO! *NO! NOOOOO!*'

Everyone stopped. The silence was deafening.

'Listen to me,' said Arthur. 'I got the entry form. I've eaten fifteen boxes of Crunch, and this is *my* jingle. So we're going to play is *my* way! Any questions?'

'Nope.'

'None from me.'

'Very clear.'

'Carry on.'

Arthur took a deep breath. 'Good,' he said.

'But what do we play from?' asked the Brain.

'I'll show you,' said Arthur.

He passed out some sheet music.

'There isn't much here,' said Francine. 'Just a few notes.'

'Well, it's a jingle,' said Arthur. 'The notes repeat. Now, if everyone's ready, let's give it everything we've got. One, two, and —'

Arthur motioned the band to play.

And they did.

WHRAMMMPAARROOOOO!

The strange sound shot out of Arthur's garage in all directions.

It hit Mrs Tibble first. She was walking along the pavement. The sound shook the snow from the branches overhead, covering her like sugar on a doughnut.

At the same time, Bob, the barber, was cutting Miss Tingley's hair.

WHRAMMMPAARROOOOO!

The sound blasted through the closed windows. Bob was startled – and clipped off most of her fringe.

The sound weakened at the edge of town, but it still packed a punch. Muffy's parents, the Crosswires, heard it in their living room.

Whrammmpaarrooooo!

'It's an air raid,' said Ed.

'We don't have air raids,' his wife, Millicent, reminded him.

'Well, I'm not taking any chances. We spent all that money on a bomb shelter. We may as well use it.'

And they both went down to the basement – where there was nothing more to be heard.

Chapter 6

• • • • • • • • • • •

Inside Arthur's garage, everyone stared at one another. Their mouths were wide open.

'Well,' said Arthur, 'maybe that was too much of a bang. But I think it's a good start.'

There was a knock on the garage door. Arthur opened it.

A police officer was standing outside. Her car was out on the street. The lights were flashing.

'Oh, my,' said Arthur.

'I'm investigating a complaint,' said the

officer. 'Actually, we had a number of calls.'

'You did?' said Arthur. 'What about?'

The officer looked at her notes. 'Someone thought a cat was being tortured. We take a pretty dim view of that around here. Do you have a cat?'

'No cats,' said Arthur. 'Just a dog. And he's fine. Honest.'

'Someone else heard the siren warning of a nuclear meltdown.' The officer looked over Arthur's shoulder. 'You're not using any unauthorized materials in here, are you? No uranium? No fancy isotopes?'

Arthur shook his head. 'We were just rehearsing a jingle.'

The officer scanned the band members. 'All right, then.' She put away her pad. 'Everything seems to be in order. But just a word of advice . . .'

'Yes, officer.'

'Keep the volume down. Try not to let your jingle *jangle* – if you know what I mean.'

Arthur nodded. 'I do, officer. Thank you, officer. Goodbye.'

He shut the door behind her.

'That was close,' said Buster.

Binky was looking out the window. 'She turned off the flashing lights. Too bad. Still we might make the newspaper this week.'

Arthur turned back to the others. Everyone was packing up.

'Hey! Wait! What are you doing? We'll get the tune right! Don't give up!'

'We don't want to be arrested,' said Sue Ellen.

'And I'm very busy. I am *not* building jail time into my calendar,' said Muffy.

'But the contest . . .'

The Brain sidestepped Arthur with his

cello.

'We're all going home for lunch,' said Prunella.

Francine looked at him. 'We'll come back later. I just hope you get inspired while we're gone.'

'*Very* inspired,' Muffy added.

Grandma Thora got her coat. 'Don't get discouraged, dear. It's a bit hard on the ears so far, but I'm sure you can fix that.'

The rest of the band filed out.

Arthur watched them leave. Only Buster was left.

'You'll feel better after lunch,' he said. 'I know I always think better on a full stomach.'

Arthur's stomach was in a big knot.

'I can't think about food right now. I have work to do.'

He moved towards the house.

'You should take a break, though,' said Buster.

Arthur spun around.

'Did Mozart take breaks?'

Buster didn't know. He couldn't even spell Mozart, much less comment on his schedule.

'Did the guy who wrote "Ring-Around-the-Roses" take breaks? I don't think so. They were dedicated. They were committed. And so am I.'

Chapter 7

• • • • • • • • • • • •

The knot in Arthur's stomach did not go away. It just sat there, tight and uncomfortable. Arthur tried to ignore it. He sat in his living room hunched over the piano. He stared at the keys.

The keys seemed to stare back.

Arthur played one note.

Diinnnng.

Arthur wanted to play another. But he hesitated. There were so many notes to choose from.

'*Eat Crunch*,' sang Arthur. He groaned. 'It's good, but it isn't good enough. I'll never come up with anything more.'

His head fell forwards on the keys, causing a jumble of chords to fill the air.

It was dark with his eyes closed. He opened them slowly. He could barely see through the gloom.

The fog parted up ahead, revealing a creaky bridge. It was strung with rope and wooden planks. The planks were painted white and black – like the keys of a piano. They swayed in the wind.

'That bridge doesn't look very secure,' thought Arthur. But it was the only way over the mountain pass.

D.W. was standing on the other side.

'If you want to cross safely,' she said, 'you have to play the right notes.'

'OK,' said Arthur. 'But what are they?'

His sister laughed. 'You'll find out,' she said. 'One way or another.'

Arthur frowned. He took a leap forwards, landing on the third plank.

Donnng!

'That's one small step for Arthur,' said D.W. 'Keep it up.'

Arthur jumped to a black plank.

Dinnng!

'Two for two,' said D.W.

Arthur felt better. Maybe this wouldn't be so hard. He walked on to the very next plank.

Craaccck!

'Uh-oh,' thought Arthur.

As he fell through the bridge, he could hear D.W. humming. Why couldn't she have hummed that tune earlier? It was catchy. It had a good beat. He could have played it right across the bridge.

Arthur jerked his head up. The bridge was gone. So was the mountain pass. He was back facing the piano.

But D.W. was still humming.

Arthur followed the sound into the hall. It was coming from upstairs.

Arthur tiptoed up the steps to D.W.'s room. He peeked inside.

His sister was sitting on her bed, brushing Nadine's hair. Arthur could tell that even though he couldn't see Nadine. Only D.W. could see her.

As D.W. brushed, she started to sing:

'Oh, I have a hunch
Breakfast, dinner, and lunch
Would be so fun to munch,
If I had it with Nadine!'

It was the same song she had been humming before, only now she had added the words.

Arthur's eyes bulged. It was all there right in front of him. All he had to do was change the Nadine part.

'Perfect! Just PERFECT!'

He raced back downstairs.

D.W. looked at the spot where Arthur had been standing.

'Was that Arthur?' asked Nadine.

'I think so.'

'He's definitely lost his mind,' said Nadine. 'Too much of that cereal. What's it called again?'

'Crunch,' said D.W.

'If you ask me,' said Nadine, 'he's crunched till he's out to lunch.'

They both laughed.

Chapter 8

• • • • • • • • • • • •

The mood was grim in Arthur's garage as the band members returned from lunch. The sun was setting outside, but the garage itself seemed darkened by a cloud.

Francine was tapping out a slow march on her drums.

Muffy was warming up with some painful screeches on her violin. They sounded as if she had accidentally stepped on a cat's tail.

Binky was putting a new reed in his clarinet. 'I hope everyone ate a big lunch,' he said. 'I know I did. It could be a very long afternoon.'

Even Grandma Thora seemed a little down. She was tapping her foot and singing to herself.

'Time is quickly running out,
And Arthur's on the spot,
He must put aside all doubt,
And show us what he's got.'

After each line, she wailed softly on her harmonica.

'Cheer up, everyone,' said Buster. 'I'm sure Arthur won't let us down.'

'He might not want to,' said Prunella. 'But eating all that Crunch cereal may have rotted his brain.'

Francine made a face. 'If it starts oozing out of his ears, I'm out of here.'

At that moment Arthur rushed in. His brain didn't look rotted, at least from the outside. In fact, he looked pretty happy.

'I've got it, everybody! I've got the jingle. Listen to this!'

The room grew still.

Arthur began to sing.

> *'Oh, I have a hunch*
> *Breakfast, dinner, and lunch*
> *Would be so fun to munch,*
> *If I had it with some . . .* CRUNCH!'

'It's got a good beat,' said Grandma Thora, snapping her fingers. 'And you can dance to it.'

Buster clapped. 'Way to go, Arthur!'

'Amazing!' said Francine. 'That actually was . . .'

'Good,' Muffy finished for her.

'What inspired you?' asked the Brain.

'It's hard to explain inspiration,' said Arthur. 'I was sitting in the living room. And I heard this tune . . .'

Arthur paused. He suddenly remembered where all his inspiration had come from. He lowered his eyes and fiddled with his glasses.

'I, uh, heard this tune in my head. And then . . . and then the words just came to me. That's all.'

Buster was impressed. 'Wow! I guess that's how a great jingle is born. Nothing at first . . . Nothing at second, either. And then, poof, out of nowhere – something beautiful.'

'I guess so,' said Sue Ellen.

'I've heard worse, I suppose,' said Binky.

'Good for you, Arthur,' said Grandma Thora.

Arthur bit his lip. 'Well, I'm glad everyone likes it. Now we just have to play our parts.'

He handed out some sheet music.

'We can all play and sing this together.'

He grinned. 'And if you want to add a little something, go right ahead.'

They practised for a few minutes. Everyone seemed pretty comfortable.

Arthur set up his tape recorder.

'Ready?' he asked.

Everyone nodded.

Arthur pushed the *record* button.

They played the song through – but not too loudly. Arthur shut his eyes and sang out loud and strong. When he opened his eyes, he noticed Pal jumping up and down in the yard.

'It was a good sign,' he thought.

Chapter 9

• • • • • • • • • • •

Once the tape was ready, Arthur couldn't wait to get it into the post. He sent the band home with his promise to let everyone know as soon as he heard anything.

'We're going to be rich!' said Buster.

Arthur shook his head. 'Um, Buster, the prize doesn't include any money.'

'Oh, well, we'll be famous, then. I can be flexible.'

He tooted twice on his tuba and headed for home.

Arthur went into the house to get the package ready. He wrote a quick letter and put it in an envelope with the tape.

Grandma Thora helped him work out how many stamps he needed.

Then he went back outside.

'Where are you going, Arthur?' asked D.W.

She and Nadine were playing in the snow.

'Can't talk now, D.W. I'm in a hurry.'

His sister spotted the package under his arm. 'Ooooh! Is that the jingle for the contest? I heard you playing something before.'

Arthur looked down at the package.

'This? Oh, yes, I suppose so.'

'So, what did you come up with? Let's hear it.'

'You don't have to be polite, D.W. I know you and Nadine aren't interested.'

'Nadine doesn't like it when you put words in her mouth, Arthur. She likes to decide things for herself.'

'Good for her,' said Arthur. 'But, really,

I'm in a —'

D.W. frowned. 'You like the song, don't you?'

'Oh, yes. Very much.'

'Well, sing it to me.'

'Oh . . . munch . . . crunch . . . snap, crackle, pop . . . something like that. Oops, look at the time. I don't want to miss the last post.'

D.W. would have said more, but Arthur was no longer there to hear it.

D.W. turned back to Nadine. Sometimes her brother was more than a little strange. She shrugged, hoping it wasn't contagious.

As Arthur headed down the street, he slowed to a walk. He had avoided telling D.W. where the jingle had come from. Of course, she didn't even know she had helped him. So there was no reason to tell her. Not really. Great artists were always taking inspiration from the people and places around them.

Arthur was on stage at a concert in the park. He was sitting in front of a piano. A cheering crowd could be heard in the background. He played the theme to the jingle and flashed a big grin. The crowd cheered.

Many rows back, D.W. was pushing her way to the stage.

'Arthur! Arthur! I know that song. Did you tell them the truth?'

Arthur heard his sister's voice but couldn't see her.

'D.W., where are you?'

D.W. had almost reached the stage, but before she could climb the stairs, several people rushed forwards to block her way.

'Who was that?' asked the beefy head of security.

'Oh, just one of my many fans,' said Arthur. 'Some of them can be very determined.'

Arthur sighed. He had arrived at the postbox. All he had to do was drop in the envelope. Nothing to it, really. But somehow he couldn't. Not yet. He just stood there, blinking in the sunlight.

Chapter 10

• • • • • • • • • • • •

On Saturday morning two weeks later, D.W. and Arthur were watching TV in their pyjamas.

'*Will the Bionic Bunny be able to defeat Captain Junk Food? We'll find out after these adverts.*'

'Captain Junk Food is pretty powerful,' said D.W. 'I think the Bionic Bunny has his hands full.'

'Could be,' said Arthur. 'And the show is making me hungry.'

He headed for the kitchen – but stopped suddenly as a song came from the TV.

'Oh, I have a hunch
Breakfast, dinner and lunch . . .'

Arthur turned to see a Crunch nugget in a tuxedo singing into a microphone.

'Would be so fun to munch
If I had it with some . . . CRUNCH!'

D.W. yawned. 'This advert isn't as good as the old one – hey, wait a minute . . .'

Arthur raced to the TV and stood in front of it.

'D.W., I can explain everything.'

His sister folded her arms. 'You'd better,' she said.

'Calm down in there,' said their father, poking his head out from the kitchen. 'Breakfast is ready. It's my special porridge. Fibre is its middle name.'

D.W. switched off the TV and headed for the kitchen. Arthur followed.

The table was set with bowls of industrial-strength porridge.

'You see,' said Arthur. 'I was going to tell you. I mean, at first I wasn't. But I never posted that entry. I did it again. But I still didn't tell you . . . I was convinced I'd lose – I mean, you'd lose.'

D.W. rolled her eyes. 'Arthur, you're making even less sense than usual. What's going on?'

'You'll love this stuff,' said Mr Read. 'One bowl – and you won't be hungry till dinner.'

He tapped the porridge with a spoon.

'In fact, you may not even be able to move till dinner.'

'The contest!' Arthur went on. 'I didn't tell you because —'

'Tell me what?'

'That I —'

He was interrupted by the doorbell.

'Who could that be?' said Mr Read.

He went to the front door and opened it. A delivery man stood outside. He was wearing a hat shaped like a bowl of cereal.

'Is this the Read residence?'

'Yes?' Mr Read said cautiously.

The man cleared his throat. 'On behalf of the Crunch Cereal Company, I am happy to present you with a year's supply of Crunch cereal.'

He motioned to his partner, who dropped a huge crate onto the Reads' driveway.

'We also have a certificate proclaiming the winner of the Crunch Cereal Jingle Contest.'

Mr Read looked overwhelmed. 'And that is?'

'Ms D.W. Read.'

'Me?' said D.W.

Arthur sighed. 'That's what I was trying

to tell you.'

A little later the whole family was gathered outside.

'I wanted to tell you that I sent your song in,' said Arthur. 'But I didn't want you to get your hopes up. You aren't angry are you?'

D.W. just laughed. 'You sent that stupid thing in? And it won?' She beamed. 'Of course, I have much better songs than that!'

'Oh, really?' said Arthur. 'Such as?'

D.W. smiled. 'Well, there's the one I wrote this morning:

> *Oh, everyone thinks*
> *that my brother stinks*
> *like a piece of yellow cheese!*
> *But me, I say,*
> *that he's OK*
> *as long as there's a breeze.'*

'D.W.!'

His sister started to run. Arthur chased after her.

'Come back here,' he said. 'I'll show you who stinks. But don't step on the cereal.'

'Moooom.'

'Daaaad!'

Their parents sighed.

'Who's going to eat all this cereal?' asked Mr Read.

Mrs Read pointed to Arthur and D.W., who were now pelting each other with snowballs. 'They will. Don't you see? They're working on their appetites.'

'Oh,' said Mr Read. 'In that case, let's leave them to it.'

Then they both went back inside, closing the door behind them.